# Andi's Lonely Little Foal

## Circle C Beginnings Series

*Andi's Pony Trouble*
*Andi's Indian Summer*
*Andi's Fair Surprise*
*Andi's Scary School Days*
*Andi's Lonely Little Foal*
*Andi's Circle C Christmas*

Circle C Beginnings

# Andi's Lonely Little Foal

Susan K. Marlow

Illustrated by Leslie Gammelgaard

*Andi's Lonely Little Foal*


Published by Kregel Publications, a division of Kregel, Inc., P.O. Box 2607, Grand Rapids, MI 49501.



ISBN 978-0-8254-4185-1

Printed in the United States of America
11 12 13 14 15 / 5 4 3 2 1

# Contents

# New Words

| | |
|---|---|
| **bellow** | to make a loud, deep noise |
| **grain** | seeds like corn and oats; food for cows and horses |
| **grandfather clock** | a tall clock that stands on the floor |
| **hitching post** | a post or railing where people tie up horses to "park" them |
| **hooves** | a horse's or cow's feet |
| **nicker** | a friendly horse greeting |
| **nuzzle** | when a horse rubs or pushes gently with its nose |
| **señorita** | the Spanish word for "Miss" |
| **slingshot** | a Y-shaped stick with stretchy rubber tied to the ends; used to throw small stones |
| **yippee-ki-yay!** | what the cowboys yell to round up the cattle |

## Chapter 1

# The Not-So-Good Idea

"A penny for your thoughts, Andi," Justin said at breakfast one Saturday morning.

Andi looked up. Sometimes big brothers said confusing things.

Like right now.

"A penny?" Andi wrinkled her eyebrows. "For what?"

But she perked up. A penny could buy lemon drops. Or taffy candy.

*Yum!*

Justin laughed. "I just meant that I want to know what you're thinking. You're very quiet this morning."

Justin was right about that. Andi always tried to be quiet at the table.

That was the rule. Grown-ups talked. Children were quiet.

Unless somebody spoke to them first.

Justin was already grown up. So was Chad. And Mitch nearly was. They always had lots to talk about, so Andi had lots of practice being quiet.

No talking at the table made it easy for Andi to daydream.

Andi liked to daydream about riding Taffy someday. When her baby horse grew up. Andi dreamed about riding Taffy in a real race.

Taffy would win, of course! Then everybody would clap.

And Andi would win a blue ribbon.

*Hooray for Taffy!*

Only right now, Andi's daydreams were not so enjoyable. A boy named Johnny was picking on her at school.

Andi could not get thoughts of that mean bully out of her head.

"A penny for your thoughts," Justin said again.

He laid a penny next to Andi's plate of pancakes.

Andi looked around the breakfast table. Her

mother and sister and brothers were all waiting. And smiling.

Even bossy Chad was smiling.

"I was thinking about Johnny," Andi said at last. "He's the meanest boy in the whole entire school. He's only eight, but he's meaner than the big boys."

"Johnny is a bully," Andi's big sister Melinda said.

"He's got a slingshot," Andi said in a rush. She didn't want Melinda to tell everything. "At recess he finds acorns and tries to hit birds. And he chews paper and—"

Andi made a face. "He shoots *disgusting* spitballs with that thing."

Johnny was mean in other ways too. He chased the girls with snakes. He put frogs in the water bucket. He pushed children down.

He even pushed Andi down once.

But Andi pulled his hair after that. Now Johnny left her alone.

Some of the time.

Andi knew Mother would not like to hear about the hair-pulling. It was not ladylike to pull hair. Not even a bully's hair.

So Andi didn't say that part out loud.

Instead, she picked up the penny and said, "I'm not scared of that mean Johnny. Not even a teensy bit."

"Then why are you thinking about him?" Chad asked.

Andi shrugged. "I don't know. I can't stop."

Chad grinned. "I know what will help you stop thinking about mean boys."

"What?" Andi asked.

"I have something important to do," he said. "And I need your help."

Andi didn't answer.

Sometimes Chad needed help with chores. Like cleaning out her pony's stall. Or picking weeds from Mother's flower garden. Or filling the wood box.

Andi did not want to do chores this morning. She wanted to play with Taffy.

So she just looked at Chad. She didn't even smile.

"You can help me take Taffy away from Snowflake," Chad told her. "It's time she grew up."

Andi's mouth fell open. *Take Taffy away from her mama?*

"No!" she hollered, jumping up from her chair. "Taffy's too little!"

"Andrea," Mother said, "please do not shout at the table."

Andi slumped back into her seat. "Sorry, Mother."

"Taffy is big and strong," Chad said. "She doesn't need her mother's milk anymore."

Andi scowled when she heard that.

Chad kept talking. "Taffy's been away from Snowflake before. Don't you remember? You and Riley got lost and ended up with the Indians."

"But that was just for one night," Andi said. "And when we got home, Taffy wouldn't leave Snowflake. She didn't even want me to lead her around. Not for a long time."

Andi took a deep breath. "So I don't think she wants to try that idea again."

"She's ready to do this," Chad said. He was not smiling now.

"Taffy is my very own horse," Andi huffed. "I get to decide when she's ready to do things."

"No, little sister," Chad said. "*I* decide when she's ready."

Andi felt all shivery inside. Poor Taffy! She would be lonely for her mother.

"Please wait a little bit longer," Andi begged.

Chad shook his head. "I have time this weekend. It will only take a few days."

"But—" A big lump was sticking in Andi's throat.

Chad stood up. He dropped his napkin on the table.

"You can help me, Andi," he said. "Or you can stay out of my way. It's your choice."

*I don't like that choice!* Andi thought.

But she kept the talking back to herself.

## Chapter 2

# Taffy

Chad left the dining room.

Andi knew where her big brother was going. He was going to the barn. He would take Snowflake outside, far away from Taffy.

Taffy would be left all alone in her stall.

The lump in Andi's throat grew bigger. Her eyes started to sting.

*No crying!*

"Eat your breakfast, Andrea," Mother said.

Andi took a bite of her half-eaten pancakes. They were cold. And squishy. And sticky with syrup.

*Yuck!*

Andi wasn't hungry anymore. Bossy Chad had spoiled her breakfast.

Melinda finished eating and asked to be excused. Then Justin left the table.

Finally, Andi's brother Mitch ate the last pancake. He took his dishes to the kitchen.

Mother and Andi were left sitting at the table.

"Why can't Taffy stay with Snowflake a little bit longer?" Andi asked. "It wouldn't hurt anything."

"Taffy is old enough to leave Snowflake," Mother said. "There is no reason to wait."

"But she'll cry for her mama," Andi said.

She picked up a napkin and wiped the syrup off her chin. Then she wiped away the tears that had sneaked out of her eyes.

She hoped Mother didn't see those drippy tears.

"Chad knows a lot more about horses than you do," Mother said. "You need to trust him. He knows what's best for Taffy."

Andi stared at her soggy pancakes. Mother was not on her side. Not today.

She wasn't on Taffy's side either.

Mother pushed back her chair and stood up.

That meant the talking was over.

"I think Chad would still like your help," Mother said. "Take your dishes to the kitchen then run and find him. Melinda can gather the eggs today."

Andi felt a little better when she heard that. For once she didn't have to tiptoe past that mean old rooster to get the eggs.

Today, Henry the Eighth would be Melinda's problem.

She smiled a little. "Yes, Mother."

Andi left her dishes in the kitchen and ran out the back door.

Halfway to the barn, she saw her friend Riley. He was dumping a pan of water off the cookhouse porch. The water splashed onto the dusty ground.

"Hey, Andi!" Riley yelled.

He set the pan down and ran over. "Let's get our lassos and find the dogs. We can practice roping them."

Andi gave Riley a big smile. She suddenly had an idea.

An *excellent* idea.

And it was not about roping the dogs with a lasso.

Riley could talk to Chad about Taffy and Snowflake!

Riley was eight years old. Two whole years older than Andi. He was smart too. He knew a lot about horses.

Riley would know just what to say to Chad.

But Riley's eyes got big when Andi told him about Taffy.

His eyes got even bigger when she asked him to talk to Chad.

"Are you crazy?" Riley said. "Cook already got after me this morning. I don't want your brother mad at me too."

That's when Andi remembered that Riley was a little bit scared of Chad.

"Sorry, Riley," she said.

It was no fun to be scolded by the grumpy ranch cook. It was no fun to be scolded by Chad either.

Just then, Chad poked his head out the barn door.

"Taffy and I sure could use your help, Andi," he said. "What did you decide?"

Andi scowled. She wanted to tell Chad to leave Taffy and Snowflake alone. She wanted to stomp her foot and tell him he was not the boss.

But Andi did not say those rude words to her brother. Not this time.

She didn't want Chad to carry her back to the house upside down. She didn't want Mother to scold her for talking back.

Andi let out a big breath. It was hard to say the right words.

*Very* hard.

But she walked over to Chad and made those words come out. "I want to help."

Chad smiled at her. "Good. I'll take Snowflake out to the pasture. You and Riley stay inside and keep Taffy company."

Taffy gave a happy nicker when she saw Andi. She swished her creamy white tail. She nuzzled Andi's shoulder. She nibbled Andi's hair.

She didn't seem to care that her mama was gone.

Then Andi brushed Taffy. She had to stand on an upside-down bucket to do it. Her foal was getting so tall!

Taffy stood very still. She liked to be brushed.

"Taffy thinks today is the same as every day," Andi told Riley. "Maybe she won't care that Snowflake's not coming back."

Riley rubbed Taffy's nose.

"I think Taffy is in for a big surprise," he said.

## Chapter 3

# Lasso Fun

A few minutes later, Chad came back inside the barn. He leaned over the half-door of Taffy's stall.

"You can play with Taffy all day long," he told Andi. "Take Coco and go riding. Taffy can go too."

Andi's eyes got big. "I can play with Taffy all day? No chores?"

"*This* is your chore," Chad said. "Just make sure you keep Taffy away from Snowflake."

He winked at Andi and left.

"Lucky you," Riley said. "I wish Uncle Sid would give *me* chores like that."

Andi giggled. That sounded funny—playing with horses for a chore.

"I like this new chore," she said.

Andi put a halter around Taffy's head. Then she opened the stall door.

"I'll get Coco ready for you," Riley said.

Coco was a pokey old pony. But Andi was happy to ride him if Taffy could come along.

Soon, she was sitting on her pony in the sunny yard. Taffy stayed close to Coco. They touched noses and whinnied.

*Good morning!* they seemed to be saying.

Riley sat on his horse, Midnight. He was making big loops in his rope.

"Guess what, Andi," he said. "I can lasso a dog at the same time I'm riding Midnight."

Andi's eyebrows went up. "No, you can't!"

Andi had tried and tried, but she could never rope those dogs. Not even when she was standing only ten steps away.

"I can too!" Riley said. "Let's call the dogs. You'll see."

Andi frowned. Sometimes Riley acted too big for his britches. He could do tricks on Midnight. But could he *really* lasso the dogs?

Maybe Riley was just talking big.

Andi yelled for the ranch dogs. "Duke! Prince! King! Here, boys!"

Riley whistled and called the dogs too.

Three big dogs ran out from behind the barn. They raced over to Andi, barking. Their tongues hung out. They wagged their tails and ran around in circles.

One yellow dog jumped up and licked Andi's boot.

"Get down, Duke," Andi said. She did not like dog kisses . . . not even on her foot.

Duke nipped Coco's leg and barked. He wanted to play.

Coco did not kick Duke for biting him. He just looked at the dog. Nothing ever upset that pokey old pony.

Andi kicked Coco's sides. "Go fast," she told her pony. "As fast as you can."

Coco trotted across the yard. Taffy followed close behind.

So did the dogs.

They ran back and forth, barking. They chased Taffy and Coco and Midnight. They chased each other.

The ranch dogs liked to play with Andi and Riley.

Andi watched Riley trot on Midnight. She laughed.

Riley looked so funny! He bounced up and down on his big black horse. He was swinging the lasso over his head. The rope looked a little wobbly.

Andi laughed harder. "You can't lasso a dog with a wobbly rope!"

Then Riley's rope flew out. It dropped over King's head.

Just like that.

King sat down fast.

Andi stopped laughing. She yanked Coco to a standstill.

"You did it!" she shouted, very surprised.

Riley was *not* talking big. He really could lasso a dog!

Riley slid off Midnight. He knelt down and gave King a big hug. "Good boy!"

Then Riley pulled the rope off. He ruffled King's shiny black fur.

"You're the best dog in all of California!" he said.

King's tongue came out. He licked Riley's face. His tail thumped the dusty ground.

Andi got down from Coco and hugged King too. But she didn't let him lick her face.

"That's pretty good," she told Riley. "When did you learn to do it? And how come I never saw you practice?"

"I practiced when you were at school," Riley said. "I wanted to surprise you."

Andi crossed her arms and huffed. "No fair! You get to work on the ranch. I have to go to school."

"Don't worry, Andi," Riley said. "When my mother gets well, I'll go home. Then I'll go back to school too."

He stood up. "But right now I like working on your ranch. Most days, anyway. When Uncle Sid or Cook don't give me too many chores."

Riley wound his lasso into loops and walked over to Midnight.

"I've practiced on the dogs long enough," he said. "I'm ready to lasso a calf."

"A *calf*?" Andi's heart started to thump. "A calf is too big and too wild to lasso. Chad will skin you alive if you try."

At least, that's what Chad told Andi he would do if *she* ever tried to rope a calf.

Mostly it meant he would yell and yell.

Riley climbed up on Midnight. "I wasn't thinking about the wild cattle."

Andi wrinkled her eyebrows. "What other calves are there?"

Riley pointed to the big pasture behind the cookhouse.

"The milk cow has a calf," he said. "Just my size. I'm going to lasso *him*."

## Chapter 4

# Lasso Trouble

Andi didn't say a word. She shaded her eyes and looked where Riley was pointing.

Far away, behind the cookhouse, three brown cows were eating grass. A brown-and-white calf was jumping and playing next to the cows. He wasn't very old, but he looked bigger than the dogs.

A lot bigger.

Andi gulped. "Are you sure you can rope that calf?"

"Yep," Riley said. "Chad told us to go riding. Let's ride in the back pasture."

"Okay." Andi grabbed Coco's mane. She pulled herself up onto her pony. "But I still don't think you can lasso a calf."

Maybe Riley was just talking big again.

Riley laughed. "That calf is a lot bigger than King. How can I miss?"

He turned Midnight toward the back pasture. Andi followed on Coco. Taffy kicked up her hooves and galloped to catch up.

It was easy to get into the pasture. Riley could open the gate without climbing down from his horse.

The cows didn't even look up when Andi and Riley rode near them. They were not wild cattle. They were tame and gentle milk cows. Riley milked one of them every morning and every night.

Cook always milked the other two cows.

Andi sat on Coco and waited for Riley to get his lasso ready. She watched Taffy gallop across the field. Her foal was fast as the wind!

Andi's heart did a happy skip. Taffy's curly little mane and tail were long and silky now. Her pale yellow coat had turned bright gold.

Taffy looked like a shiny gold piece in the sunshine.

"Here I go! Yippee-ki-yay!"

Riley's cowboy yell crashed into Andi's happy thoughts.

The cows looked up. They shook their horns.

Riley's shout brought the dogs running too.

King, Duke, and Prince leaped through the rail fence. They ran after Riley and Midnight, barking and yapping.

The cows mooed and started to run. The calf ran.

"Catch him, Riley!" Andi shouted.

Riley chased the little calf around the pasture.

The calf was fast, but Midnight was faster. That smart horse knew just what to do to keep Riley next to the calf.

Then Riley threw his lasso.

*Plunk!* It hit the ground.

Andi groaned. "Oh, too bad! You missed."

Just then Riley's rope jerked. With a yelp, he went flying off Midnight.

Riley had missed the calf's head. But he had caught one hoof.

One hoof was enough.

The calf hollered for his mama and kept running. He dragged Riley across the grass.

Riley held onto his rope, yelling at the calf to stop.

The dogs barked louder. They chased Riley and the calf.

Mama Cow bellowed and ran after them all.

Andi could not stop laughing. What a noise! Yelling and mooing and barking and bellowing.

But Riley had done it. He had lassoed that calf.

"Hooray!" Andi shouted. She clapped and clapped. "You did it!"

Then Riley let go of the rope.

The calf kept running.

Mama Cow kept running.

The dogs kept running and barking.

Andi laughed until tears rolled down her cheeks. Then she slid off Coco and ran over to Riley.

Riley was lying on the ground, very still.

Andi bent down next to him.

"Are you okay?" she asked, wiping away her tears.

Riley sat up. He looked a little shaky. His hat was gone. His face was covered with dirt and grass. So was his shirt. And his pants.

"I'm fine," he said with a grin. "I lassoed my first calf."

Then he sighed. "But how am I ever going to get my rope back?"

Andi didn't answer. She was staring across the field.

Suddenly, Andi stood up.

"Here comes Cook," she said. "He looks mad. Maybe roping the calf was not a good idea."

Cook stomped across the field. He was carrying a small can of grain. And he was yelling in Spanish.

That meant he was *very* angry.

Riley's smiley face turned scared. He jumped to his feet and tried to brush the dirt off his clothes.

"Cook's going to skin me alive," he said in a shaky voice.

Cook shook the can and called the cows. They came running. They always ran fast when Cook shook the grain can.

Then Cook bent over and held the calf's foot. He slid the lasso off. He did not give the rope back to Riley.

"You are in a heap of trouble, boy," Cook growled in English. "I will find plenty of chores to keep you busy." His dark eyes glared at Riley.

Cook's eyes were glaring at Andi too. "And you, *señorita*, stay away from here. Leave these cows alone."

"Yes, Cook," Andi whispered. She looked at the ground.

Nothing was worse than being scolded by the grumpy ranch cook.

But then Riley said something *much* worse. "Where's Taffy?"

## Chapter 5

# Up, Up, and Over!

Andi spun around. She could not see Taffy. Not anywhere in the whole entire pasture!

"I see her," Cook said.

Cook had good, sharp eyes. Even if they were almost hidden under his bushy black eyebrows.

"She is galloping along the back fence," Cook said. "Over by the trees."

Now Andi could see Taffy. She looked small. Like a golden dog instead of a golden horse.

And that wasn't all Andi saw.

Snowflake was galloping too. Right next to Taffy. Only, Snowflake was on her own side of the fence.

Snowflake gave a loud whinny and galloped faster. She wanted her baby.

Taffy whinnied back. It looked like Taffy wanted her mama too.

"Taffy!" Andi shouted. "Come back here!" She scrambled up on Coco and kicked him hard. "Go fast, Coco!"

But Coco did *not* go fast. He trotted. Like always.

Just then, Riley galloped past Andi. He caught up to Taffy before Andi did. Midnight was fast.

But not fast enough.

Snowflake jumped up . . . up . . . up.

Then over the fence she went.

"Oh, no!" Andi yelled.

Taffy galloped over and began to drink her mother's warm milk. Her tail swished. Snowflake's tail swished too. They looked happy to see each other.

Andi was glad about that. But she knew Chad would not be happy.

*Keep Taffy away from Snowflake, Andi!*

A shiver went down Andi's neck when she remembered her brother's words.

"You better take Taffy back to her stall," Riley said when Andi trotted up. "Before Chad sees what happened."

Riley was right about that. Andi did not want her brother to find out about this.

When Chad was mad, he could really yell!

"How do we get Snowflake back in her own pasture?" Andi asked.

Snowflake would not want to leave Taffy. And probably nobody could make her. Snowflake was too big.

Riley held up his lasso.

"Cook gave my rope back, after Snowflake jumped the fence," he said. "I'll tie her up. You take Taffy out of sight. Then I'll lead Snowflake back to her own pasture."

Andi clapped her hands. "That's a jim-dandy idea, Riley! You're my best friend ever."

Then she looked at the cookhouse, far away. Cook was gone.

"Do you think Cook will tell Chad what happened?" she asked.

Riley shrugged his shoulders. "Cook is too busy to bother Chad. He's finding chores for me."

He sighed. "Besides, I think Cook likes to hand out his own punishments."

"I hope so," Andi said.

It was easy as pie to call Taffy now. Her belly was full of warm milk. She was ready to play again. She followed Andi and Coco out of the pasture and into the barn.

Andi did not see Riley for the rest of the day. She stayed far away from the cookhouse.

Cook was finding heaps of chores for Riley. Andi did not want Cook to find heaps of chores for her too.

Taffy was Andi's chore today, and it was a big chore.

Bigger than Andi thought.

Taffy whinnied every time Andi left her alone. Sometimes Taffy banged against the stall door. She wanted out!

Coco was in the next stall. But Taffy did not care about Coco now. She wanted Andi. Or Snowflake.

When Andi ate lunch, she could hear Taffy's whinnies.

Andi ate fast.

But not so fast that Mother would scold her for having bad table manners.

After lunch, Andi took carrots and apples to Taffy. She took a lump of sugar. Just one. That's all the sugar Mother would let Andi have.

She took her reading book to the barn too.

Andi gave Taffy the apples and carrots. She fed her the lump of sugar.

Taffy gobbled up the sugar. Then she nibbled Andi's hair. Taffy's nibbles felt like a big thank-you.

"You're welcome," Andi said with a giggle.

Then she sat down in the straw and opened her reader.

"This is the only book I know how to read," Andi told Taffy.

She took a big breath and read, "Is it an ax? It is an ax. It is my ax. It is by me. So it is! I go to it."

Andi slammed the book shut.

"Who wants to read about an *ax*?" she grouched. "I wish I could read a dime novel. They're full of adventure."

Taffy stamped her foot. It looked like she didn't like that story either. It looked like she wanted to go out and play.

But too bad for Taffy. Playtime was over. It was getting late.

Soon, Andi would have to go inside for the night.

Then Taffy would be all alone.

Chapter 6

# Night Noises

Andi sat on the back porch. Her eyes stung. A big lump was stuck in her throat.

Every time Taffy whinnied, tears leaked out of Andi's eyes.

Taffy wanted her mother.

The back door opened.

Andi jumped up and rubbed her eyes. Chad was looking down at her.

It was hard to talk with a lump in her throat, but Andi said, "Taffy is so sad."

"I know," Chad said. "The first night is always the hardest. After tonight it will get better."

Andi didn't know how that could be true. Taffy's whinnies sounded terrible!

"Can't Snowflake stay with Taffy one more night?" she begged. "Please? I promise I won't ask again."

But Chad said no.

"In a few days it will be over," he told her. "Taffy won't want her mother anymore. You'll see. I'm doing the best thing for Taffy. You just have to trust me."

Andi pouted. How could she trust Chad when Taffy was crying so much?

"You're just being bossy," she said. "Like always. You don't even care that Taffy is sad!"

Chad did not get angry. Instead, he smiled and ruffled Andi's hair.

"Mother wants you to come inside," he said. "It's past your bedtime."

Andi went up to bed, but she wasn't sleepy. She said her prayers. She counted to one hundred. She tried to sleep.

But she could not stop thinking about Taffy.

Andi lay in bed a long time. Her eyes were wide open. So were her ears.

She heard the big grandfather clock downstairs.

*Bong, bong, bong . . .*

The clock struck eleven times.

Andi listened some more. Her room was too far away from the barn. She could not hear Taffy's whinnies.

But Andi knew Taffy was unhappy. And scared. And lonely.

Andi sniffed. Then she got an idea. It was not her best idea ever.

Mostly because it was a scary idea.

"But I have to do it," Andi whispered to herself. "I just have to."

So Andi slid out of bed. She pulled on her shirt, overalls, and boots. She put on her jacket. Then she grabbed a blanket and rolled it up.

Andi tiptoed down the stairs and into the kitchen. A lamp was turned down low. There was just enough light to keep Andi from crashing into something.

Crashing into things would not be good. Somebody might hear the sound and wake up.

*Creak!*

The back door made only a little noise. Soon Andi was standing on the porch.

She shivered. Andi did not like the dark.

Not even a teensy bit. She was glad a full moon was shining. It lit up the whole yard.

*Well, most of the yard,* Andi thought. She peeked at the dark shadows under the trees.

Across the yard, the barn looked like a shadowy giant. The hayloft windows were black eyes. The barn doors covered up a big, scary mouth.

Andi gulped.

"A pretend mouth," she told herself.

Inside that shadowy barn, Taffy was whinnying. Loudly.

Taffy's cries made Andi forget about the dark. She even forgot about being scared.

Taffy needed her!

Andi held her blanket tightly. She ran across the yard and into the barn.

Moonlight was shining through the barn windows.

Andi was glad about that. It made it easy to find Taffy's stall.

Andi reached up high to open the half-door. Then she stepped into the stall.

"Here I am, Taffy," she called to her foal.

Right away Taffy stopped whinnying. She nickered a happy greeting and nuzzled Andi.

Andi was happy to see Taffy too. Being with Taffy made the nighttime barn seem almost friendly.

A few minutes later, Taffy gave a sleepy grunt and lay down.

Andi was tired too. She spread her blanket on the straw. Then she curled up beside Taffy's warm body.

"Good night, Taffy," she whispered, yawning.

Andi closed her eyes. The straw rustled under her. Taffy's warm breath blew softly on her head.

Then . . .

*Scratch, scratch, scratch!*

Andi's eyes flew open. Her heart skipped a beat. She sat up and threw her arms around Taffy's neck.

"What's that noise?" she asked in a shaky voice.

Taffy's ears twitched, and she lifted her head.

Andi looked up too. Her thumpy heart slowed down.

A barn cat was sharpening his claws on the top edge of the half-door.

He jumped down, walked over to Andi, and rubbed his head on her leg. He was purring.

Andi giggled. She pulled the tabby cat close and petted him. The cat purred louder.

Andi lay down. Everything felt warm and cozy now. She didn't feel scared. Not anymore.

*Thank you, God, for this friendly kitty,* she prayed.

When Andi closed her eyes this time, she fell asleep.

Just like that.

## Chapter 7

# Sunday Is Not a School Day

*Cock-a-doodle-doo!*

Andi jerked awake when the rooster crowed. She sat up and rubbed her eyes. Early morning light was peeking through the window of Taffy's stall.

The tabby cat was gone. Taffy was standing up.

Quick as a wink, Andi jumped up.

"I have to go inside," she told Taffy. "I have to get ready for church. But I'll dress fast. I'll eat fast too, and come right back. Coco is here. You can touch noses. Please don't cry when I leave."

But even if Taffy whinnied, there was nothing Andi could do about it.

Andi rushed out of the barn. When she passed the chicken coop, she waved.

"Thanks for waking me up," she told Henry the Eighth.

*That mean old rooster is finally good for something*, she thought.

A few minutes later, Andi was back in her room. She pulled off her overalls. She wiggled into a Sunday dress.

Mother walked in just in time to button Andi's dress.

"You're up already," she said with a smile. "Good. We must hurry this morning."

"Why?" Andi asked.

Mother tied a wide blue sash around Andi's waist.

"Because they are starting a Sunday school for you children," she said. "We have to leave early to be on time."

Sunday. School. Those two words did not belong together.

"Sunday isn't a school day," Andi said, frowning. "I go to school all week."

Mother laughed. "Sunday school is different from school. You will like it."

Andi was not sure about that.

"I want to see Taffy before we go," she said. "Please?"

Mother brushed Andi's hair and tied it back with a blue bow.

"There won't be time for that," she told Andi. "Taffy will be fine. She has Coco for company."

"She doesn't want Coco," Andi grouched. "She wants me. Or Snowflake."

"Andrea," Mother said in her warning voice.

That meant, *No talking back.*

So Andi stopped talking. But she didn't stop thinking.

*I don't want to go to Sunday school!*

⇾ ⇽

Sunday school was in a corner of the big, white church. A dozen children sat on benches, waiting.

Andi sat down too. Her friend Cory waved at her. Everybody smiled.

Everybody except that mean boy, Johnny. He stuck his tongue out at Andi.

Andi wanted to stick her tongue out at Johnny too.

But she didn't do it. Not with Melinda sitting next to her.

"Welcome to Sunday school, boys and girls," the teacher said. She was young and pretty. "My name is Miss Brady. The first thing we're going to do is learn a new song."

Andi perked up. Maybe Sunday school would not be too bad. Not if they could sing!

The new song was called "Jesus Loves Me."

Andi loved that song right from the start. She learned it in no time. She sang, "Yes, Jesus loves me! The Bible tells me so!" louder than any of the other children.

Andi liked the Bible story too. Even if she already knew it.

She knew the story about Jesus and the little children by heart. But Andi liked to hear that Jesus loved her just as much as He loved her big sister and grown-up brothers.

Mother was right. Andi liked everything about this new Sunday school. Miss Brady smiled all the time. She helped the children learn a Bible verse. She let them ask questions.

Andi was surprised when Miss Brady said, "Sunday school is almost over."

It had gone by very fast!

"It's time to pray," Miss Brady said. "Does anyone have a prayer request—something they would like us all to talk to God about?"

Two hands went up.

"Pray for the missionaries in faraway Africa," one girl said.

"And in China," a boy added.

Andi's heart was thumping fast. Her stomach felt tickly. She wanted to raise her hand too. She had a request for God. An important one.

Andi waited until everyone else had said their prayer requests. Then she raised her hand.

"Please pray for my foal named Taffy," she said. "Chad took her away from her mother. She's very sad and lonely. I want God to help her not feel so lonely."

Nobody said a word.

Then Andi heard a giggle.

And that mean Johnny laughed.

"You goose!" he said. "You're supposed to

pray for the preacher. Or for starving children who don't know about God."

He laughed louder. "You don't pray for *little* things . . . like a baby horse."

Andi's stomach flip-flopped. Her cheeks turned hot. She stared at her lap.

"Johnny Wilson!" Miss Brady scolded. "For

shame! God wants to hear *all* our requests. Even the little ones."

She smiled at Andi. "We'll pray for your foal first. Children, bow your heads and close your eyes."

Andi bowed her head. But she did not close her eyes.

It wasn't safe to close her eyes with Johnny in the room.

Chapter 8

# That Mean Johnny

Andi squirmed all during church. She could not sit still. Her thoughts were a jumble.

A tangled, messy jumble.

That mean ol' Johnny! *You don't pray for little things . . . like a baby horse!*

Miss Brady had sounded shocked at Johnny's words.

Andi wasn't shocked. Johnny talked mean like that all the time.

But was Johnny right? Maybe God didn't care about a lonely little foal.

"Miss Brady said God does care," Andi whispered to herself. "And she's smarter than Johnny."

But Andi's thoughts were still in a jumble.

After church, Andi wanted to go right back to the ranch. She wanted to see Taffy. She wanted to make sure her little horse was all right.

Andi looked around for her family. Justin was talking to Reverend Harris, the preacher. Mother was chatting with Miss Hall, the schoolteacher.

Andi let out a big breath. "Why do grown-ups have to stand around and talk so long?"

She wanted to tug on Mother's sleeve and say, *Hurry up!*

But she didn't do it. That would not be good manners.

Andi started walking to the family buggy.

"Maybe if Mother sees me sitting in the buggy, she will decide it's time to go home," she said to herself.

Just then Johnny stepped in front of Andi. He held up his slingshot.

"Watch this, Andi," he said, grinning.

*Whiz!* An acorn flew from the slingshot.

*Plunk!* It hit the hitching post dead center.

Johnny was a good shot.

Andi squinted at that mean boy. "Go away."

Johnny stuffed his slingshot in his back pocket. Then he crossed his arms and laughed.

"You're such a baby," he said. "Asking the Sunday school teacher to pray for a horse. That's the silliest thing I ever heard."

"Miss Brady didn't think it was silly," Andi said in a huff. "And I told you to go away. Or . . . or . . . I'll pull your hair."

Andi's fingers itched to yank that bully's hair!

"No, you won't," Johnny said. "Not with everybody looking."

Johnny was right about that.

Andi's itchy fingers grew quiet.

"Guess what," Johnny said. "I know all about weaning foals."

Andi wrinkled her eyebrows. What was Johnny talking about?

"Weaning?" she asked. "What does that mean?"

Johnny rolled his eyes.

"Don't you know *anything*?" he said. "When you take a baby horse away from its mother, it's called weaning."

Johnny came closer and whispered, "Terrible things can happen during weaning."

Andi's eyes got big. "Like what?"

"The foal whinnies and cries all the time."

"I know that," Andi said. "It's not terrible. It's just sad."

"They don't eat," Johnny said in a low, scary voice. "They get so skinny that they shrivel up. And sometimes they even *die*."

Andi swallowed hard. "That's . . . that's not true!"

"It is true," Johnny said. "On account of I saw it happen once. You can even ask my father."

Andi did not want to ask Johnny's father anything.

Johnny kept talking. "Foals can hurt themselves. They get banged up trying to get back to their mothers. Their legs can get caught in the fence. Then they go lame and can't walk."

"No!" Andi shouted.

Johnny shook his head. "You probably won't ever be able to ride that horse. Not ever, ever, ever!"

Andi's heart was pounding so hard she felt sick. Her stomach was in a tight knot.

This terrible news could not be true.

"You're acting too big for your britches!" she hollered. "You don't know everything!"

But yelling at Johnny did not make Andi feel better.

Her heart kept pounding. The knot in her stomach got tighter. And now her eyes were beginning to sting.

Andi did not want Johnny to see her cry.

"Go away!" she yelled.

Then she ran for the buggy. And she cried all by herself.

## Chapter 9

# Taffy Trouble

All the way home, Andi worried about Taffy. She sat between Mother and Chad in the big buggy and didn't say a word.

"Do you want to sit on my lap and drive the horses?" Chad asked.

Andi shook her head. Her hands were too shaky to hold the reins.

Chad's eyebrows went up. "You always want to drive. What's the matter?"

*Taffy might shrivel up and die!* Andi wanted to say.

But the words would not come out. They were too scary to say out loud.

"She's upset about Taffy," Melinda said from

the back seat. "The teacher prayed for Taffy in Sunday school."

Andi jumped up and yelled, "Be quiet, you big tattletale!"

"Andrea!" Mother scolded. She pulled Andi around and sat her down hard. "Shame on you. And on Sunday too."

Andi didn't care if it was Sunday. She didn't care about anything. Johnny's words buzzed around inside her head like mean, stinging bees.

Those bees kept stinging her thoughts until she finally sobbed, "I don't want Taffy to die!"

"What on earth?" Mother said.

Then Andi told everybody what Johnny had said.

"Is he right, Chad?" she asked, rubbing her eyes.

"Well . . ." her brother said slowly, "some things Johnny said are true. Foals cry and miss their mothers. You know that. Sometimes they stop eating."

Chad kept talking. "Sometimes a foal can hurt himself. But that hardly ever happens. Not on our ranch."

He ruffled Andi's hair. "Don't worry. You'll see that Taffy is fine."

⇢ ⇠

When Andi ran into the barn, Taffy was still whinnying. But it was not a loud whinny. It was a soft whinny. Like she had a sore throat from crying too much.

Taffy was *not* fine.

Her head hung down. Her tail was droopy. She looked very sad.

And there was a mark on her front leg.

Andi gasped. "Taffy! What happened to you?"

Quick as a wink, Andi took her foal outside. In the sunlight it looked like a big, red scrape.

"It's blood," Andi told Chad. "Taffy got hurt. We have to put her back with Snowflake. We have to keep her safe. Please!"

Chad cleaned Taffy's leg with soap and water.

"It's nothing, Andi," he said. "Taffy probably tried a little too hard to get out of her stall. It happens sometimes. There's no harm done."

He smiled. "Take Taffy and Coco out to the pasture. You can stay with her if you like."

Then Chad stopped smiling. "But Taffy is not going back with Snowflake."

Andi pouted. But she did what her brother told her.

Andi stayed with Taffy all afternoon. She fed her apples and carrots. She brushed her and talked to her.

All the time, Andi was thinking hard.

"I have to stay with you, Taffy," she said at last. "I have to keep you safe. I don't want you to get hurt again. Or go lame. Or shrivel up and die."

Shivers went up and down Andi's arms at that terrible thought.

Shivers were still going up and down Andi's arms when she went out to the barn that night. It was much colder than the night before. One blanket was not enough to keep Andi warm.

But she had to stay. She had to keep Taffy safe.

It took Andi a long time to fall asleep. She was cold, and it was a noisy night.

An owl hooted. Mice squeaked. Cats hissed. The dogs howled.

When Andi finally fell asleep, she slept and slept.

And this time when the rooster crowed, Andi did not wake up.

⇢ ⇠

"Get up, Andi."

Andi opened her eyes. Chad was standing above her. His arms were crossed. He looked grumpy.

*Very* grumpy.

"What are you doing out here?" he scolded. "It's too cold to spend the night in the barn."

"I'm keeping Taffy safe," Andi said in a small voice.

Chad shook his head.

"Take Taffy and Coco out to their pasture," he said. "Then go get ready for school."

"I have to stay home and take care of Taffy," Andi said. "It's my chore. Remember? That's what you said. Taffy is my chore."

"That was on Saturday," Chad said. He was already walking out of the barn in a big hurry.

"Today you have to go to school," he called. "Now, hurry up!"

Andi slumped against Taffy. She did not want to hurry up. She did not want to put her little horse in the pasture. Not even with Coco.

Taffy wanted Andi. Or Snowflake.

Andi rubbed Taffy's nose.

"Don't worry, Taffy," she said. "I'll make sure you don't get hurt today. You will be safe until I get home."

Then she opened Coco's stall. "Come on, Coco."

Andi led Taffy and Coco out of the barn. She took them to Snowflake's pasture.

"It's just for today," Andi told Taffy. "I'll take you back to your stall right after school."

She took a deep breath. "And Chad will never know."

## Chapter 10

# Trust Me!

"Can't we go faster?" Andi asked on the way home from school.

Justin laughed. "Are you in a hurry?" He slapped the reins across Pal's back.

The horse trotted faster.

"I'm in a big hurry," Andi said. "I want to see Taffy. She misses me."

Melinda let out a sigh. "I'm tired of hearing about—"

"Melinda," Justin said softly. That meant, *Be quiet!*

Melinda crossed her arms and slouched in the buggy. But she kept quiet all the way home.

Andi kept quiet too. She tried to feel cheerful.

*Taffy is safe with Snowflake,* she thought. *Soon she will be safe with me.*

But some not-so-cheerful thoughts kept creeping into Andi's head.

*You disobeyed. You were sneaky. It was wrong.*

Those little thoughts did not make Andi feel cheerful. They made her feel terrible.

The buggy stopped in the yard. Andi leaped out and ran to the pasture. It was a long way to run.

Andi was panting by the time she reached the fence. "Taffy!" she called.

Snowflake and Coco came running. But Taffy was not with them.

Andi frowned. Where was Taffy?

Andi raced to the barn. If Taffy was not with Snowflake and Coco, then she must be in her stall.

But Taffy was not in her stall.

Andi ran out of the barn.

*Whack!* She slammed into Riley. They both fell to the ground.

"Do you know where Taffy is?" Andi asked when she stood up.

Riley stood up too. He did not look at Andi. He kicked the dust and looked at his feet.

"She's gone," he said at last. "Chad took her away."

Andi gasped. "Where?"

Riley looked at her. "I don't know. But he was awful mad when he saw Taffy with Snowflake."

Andi blinked hard. *No crying!*

But it was no good. Andi could not keep her tears inside. Taffy was gone!

Andi ran into the house. "Mother!" she yelled.

Mother was waiting for her. She lifted Andi onto her lap and let her cry.

"Chad took Taffy away," Andi sobbed.

"I know," Mother said. "He took her to another ranch. Just for a few days. He'll bring her home when she's weaned."

"She'll be lonely!"

"Yes," Mother said sadly. "But Chad can't keep her here anymore. Not after what you did."

Andi cried louder. Those thoughts crept back into her head.

*You disobeyed. You were sneaky. It was wrong.*

"It hurts to make a foal grow up," Mother said. "But Taffy only had one or two more days to be unhappy. Then she would have been fine."

She gave Andi a hug. "When you put Taffy back with Snowflake, Chad had to start all over again. That hurt Taffy more."

"I was scared Taffy would get hurt again," Andi whispered.

"It's okay to feel scared," Mother said. "But Chad knew best. You should have trusted him even though you were scared. And you should have trusted God to take care of Taffy."

Andi rubbed her eyes and nodded. Mother was right.

"I . . . I'm sorry, Mother," Andi said at last.

Now maybe those not-so-cheerful thoughts would go away.

"I'm going to tell Chad I'm sorry too," Andi decided.

*Even if he skins me alive with his yelling.*

→ ←

Chad did not skin Andi alive with his yelling.

When she said, "I'm sorry," he hugged her.

But Chad looked sad. Like he missed Taffy even more than Andi did. Like he didn't want Taffy to be so far away from the ranch.

"Can we bring Taffy home?" Andi asked.

"You said you're sorry," he told Andi, "but you have to learn a lesson."

So Chad would not bring Taffy home.

Instead, he let Andi ride with him out to the cattle. He let her watch the cowboys lasso the calves.

Chad even showed her the hot iron that branded the calves with a big Ⓒ. That way everybody knew who the calves belonged to.

But Andi missed Taffy. A lot.

→ ←

On the next Saturday, Chad said, "I'm bringing Taffy home today. Do you want to help?"

At last!

"Yes!" Andi shouted.

Chad tossed Andi up on his horse, Sky. He sat in the saddle behind her.

"Can we gallop?" she asked.

Chad laughed. "Sure."

Sky ran fast as the wind. Faster even than Midnight. It took no time to gallop to the other ranch. Even if it was way up in the hills.

When Andi saw Taffy, she squealed and bounced up and down. Taffy looked perfectly fine. And happy.

Andi bounced right off Sky and hugged Taffy tight.

"I missed you so much," she whispered.

Taffy nickered. She nuzzled Andi's neck and nibbled her hair.

*I missed you too!* she seemed to be saying.

Then it was time to go home. Chad let Andi hold Taffy's lead rope.

They did not gallop home. Instead, they walked or trotted, so Taffy could keep up.

Andi leaned back against her brother. She didn't know why, but she felt like saying "sorry" again.

So she did.

"It was a hard lesson, little sister," Chad said. "But maybe you'll trust me next time."

He chuckled. “I do know *something* about horses, you know.”

Andi giggled. “I know.”

Chad knew something about a *lot* of things.

He even knew something about little sisters.

# A Peek into the Past

Would you like to have been a cowboy in 1874?

Books and movies make a cowboy's life sound full of adventure: A fast horse to ride. A lasso to toss around a stubborn calf. Maybe even a set of pistols hanging from your belt.

What an exciting life!

But maybe not . . .

Cowboys in 1874 worked long and hard. They lived on the ranch and slept in a bunkhouse. They took care of the rancher's cattle and horses.

When a cowboy wasn't working with the cattle, he was fixing fences. Or doing other ranch jobs—like mucking out stalls. A cowboy was busy from sunrise to sunset. He earned about a dollar a day.

A cowboy's most important tools were his horse and his rope. A hat was important too. It kept the sun off his head. It could also hold water for himself and his horse. A cowboy's boots had high heels. This kept his feet in the stirrups. But his boots were not comfortable to walk in!

A cowboy hardly ever carried a gun. A gun cost about $12.00, which was two weeks' pay. Besides, the only thing worth shooting on the ranch was a pesky rattlesnake.

Do you still want to be a cowboy?

**Susan K. Marlow**, like Andi, has an imagination that never stops! She enjoys teaching writing workshops, sharing what she's learned as a homeschooling mom, and relaxing on her 14-acre homestead in the great state of Washington.

**Leslie Gammelgaard**, blessed by the tall trees and flower gardens that surround her home in Washington state, finds inspiration for her artwork in the antics of her lively little granddaughter.

# Grow Up with Andi!

**Don't miss any of Andi's adventures in the Circle C Beginnings series**

*Andi's Pony Trouble*
*Andi's Indian Summer*
*Andi's Fair Surprise*
*Andi's Scary School Days*
*Andi's Lonely Little Foal*
*Andi's Circle C Christmas*

---

**And you can visit www.AndiandTaffy.com for free coloring pages, learning activities, puzzles you can do online, and more!**

# For readers ages 9-14!

**Andi's adventures continue in the Circle C Adventures series**

*Andrea Carter and the Long Ride Home*
*Andrea Carter and the Dangerous Decision*
*Andrea Carter and the Family Secret*
*Andrea Carter and the San Francisco Smugglers*
*Andrea Carter and the Trouble with Treasure*
*Andrea Carter and the Price of Truth*

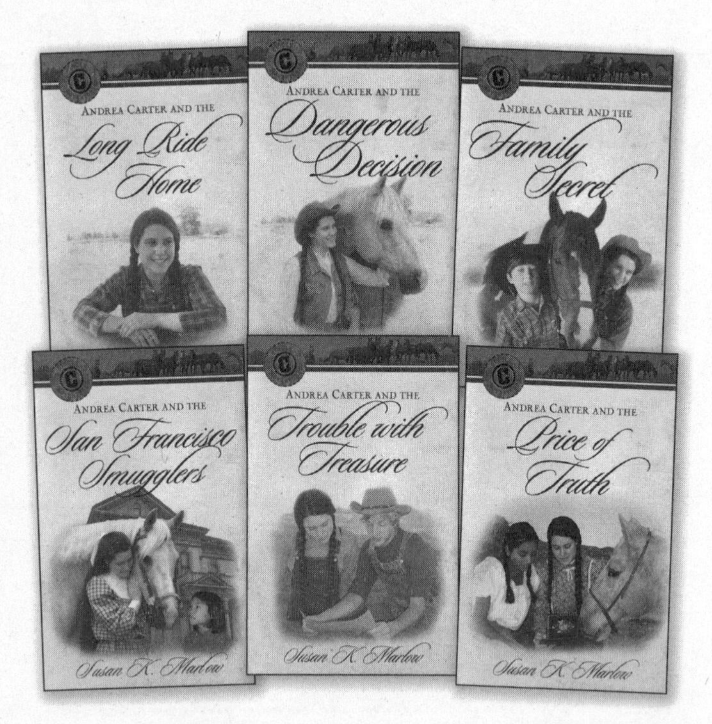


---

**Check out Andi's Web site at www.CircleCAdventures.com**